"The CSCO Chronicles is the kind of espionage series that will thrill die-hard fans of intelligence op literature who really know their stuff and tire of having to suspend their superior knowledge to enjoy a book. The author has the career experience to draw believable scenarios and masterfully utilize the lingo, and the result is a book that even those who are new to the genre will enjoy.

"This well-written spy story will keep readers entertained and in suspense with its mix of humor, danger, and fun cultural references. Protagonist Ben is a likable "regular guy" who happens to have a proclivity for languages and an overdeveloped sense of personal initiative, and we see him getting himself into trouble in scene after action-packed scene. Readers will immediately take to him and root for him throughout."

- **The 28th Annual Writer's Digest Book Awards**

"Superb. Unique. First-person narrative, lots of descriptions of solid trade-craft. Entirely believable. An homage to Adam Hall's Quiller yet in the author's entirely own voice and quite unlike anything I've read in the espionage genre. Far better than what's offered by some bigger, well-known and established names. I'm looking very much forward to further books by this author."

- **Jens Lindblad, Co-Founder of the Quiller Espionage Group**

CSCO: Venezia

The Training of a Clandestine Service Case Officer

D. A. Pendleton

A Short Story in the CSCO Chronicles

Owl Enterprises
Mooresville, NC

First Owl Enterprises trade paperback edition July 2021

Manufactured in the United States of America

10 9 8 7 6 5 4 3 2 1

Library of Congress Control Number

ISBN: 9-7985356-1292-8 (pbk)

FOREWORD

This work is the long version of the prologue to CSCO: Cutting My Teeth, the second book in the CSCO Chronicles.

It is in Beta version, published for my Beta readers to access online and anyone else interested. It still has to undergo final edits and proofreading.

What follows portrays, semi-accurately, a live training exercise between two pairs of antagonist Case Officer Candidates. Near the end of CIA's Basic Case Officer course, the Agency utilizes real-world environments, both domestically and overseas, to conduct critical training and assessment of its CO Candidates.

Clandestine surveillance is an unpredictable, chaotic combination of the grueling, frustrating, dangerous, boring, sometimes amusing, and exceptionally tedious. It taxes the very mental, emotional, and constitutional fiber of unhatched COs. It is also testament to the diligence CIA demands from its prospective officers, those charged with protecting our national security, quite often without supervision.
Enjoy!

You may e-mail me at: cscofirststation@gmail.com
Thanks again for all your feedback.

Dave Pendleton.

CSCO: VENEZIA

Chronicle:

A historical account of events arranged in order of time usually without analysis or interpretation.
- Merriam-Webster Dictionary

A factual written account of important or historical events in the order of their occurrence.
- Oxford English Dictionary

To view the first trilogy in the CSCO series, please visit:
https://cscofirststation.weebly.com/

CSCO: VENEZIA

GLOSSARY

AAR: After Action Review

Apparatchiki: Bureaucrats, in this case (Russian)

B747: Boeing 747

Cameriere: Waiter (Italian)

Carabinieri: Public Safety Police, Military or Judicial Police (Italian)

CO: Case Officer

CS: Countersurveillance

Da shto?: Say what?!

DIA: Defense Intelligence Agency

Gelatti: Ice cream (Italian)

Gondola: Gondola (Italian)

GPS / Differential GPS: Geolocating device triangulating off at least three geostationary satellites. Differential GPS combines that with a ground based location transmitter emplaced to within a few inches of accuracy.

HUMINT: Human Intelligence

Kroliki: Rabbit (Russian)

Motoscafo: Motorboat (Italian)

Palazzo: Palace (Italian)

Parisienne: Female resident of Paris (French)

POS: Piece of shit

SDR: Surveillance Detection Route

USA: U.S. Army

USAF: U.S. Air Force

Vaporetto: Water taxi (Italian)

ACKNOWLEDGMENTS

The last citation in CSCO: First Station belongs up front for this work:

Thanks to all the intrepid, nameless faces of the Clandestine Service over the years. And their support structures. Although I was never involved, I saw enough glimpses peripherally to understand the huge invisible victories that can never be credited to you publicly, and all your selfless service.

And for an aspiring first-timer, credit goes more to all the generous benefactors who recognized a meager spark that might be trainable, rather than the author himself. Thank you!

To my financial backers, scions of friendship and faith, and some devoted espionage followers, a huge thanks for your generosity—and patience:

Joan P.	San Jose, CA
Darian A.	Prague, Czech Republic
Allene W.	Monte Sereno, CA
Carla C.	Mooresville, NC
Joy F.	Williamsberg, VA
Barbara B.	Mooresville, NC
Ron L.	White Bear Lake, MN
Ilya K.	Moscow, Russia
Bill M.	Hudson, WI
Jonathan L.	New York, NY
Christian M.	Tualatin, OR
Cristina	anon

To the professional editors and my beta readers, from the unapologetic critics to the nurturing mentors, that gave of their expert time, most voluntarily, any errors or shortcomings within my prose are mine alone; your contribution and teachings were more than eye opening!: Richard W. Marek, who taught me to be brutal on myself; Mary Ellen Gavin, for her teaching, coaching, encouragement and industry insights; Kristen Weber, for her patient and insightful instruction in wordsmithing; Alyssa Hollingsworth, for her undaunting and consistent coaching and motivation; Mark Malatesta, for his high level consulting on how to eat the whole enchilada; Jill Welch, for her contribution to my progress in editing and wordsmithing; Megan Skamwell and Tara Tomczyk of Blydyn Square, for their bend-over-backwards time and advice; Joan P., a rather well-read Doctor of Electrical Engineering; and Patti P., long-time English and Literature Engineer.

A hearty thanks to my newest collaborator, Joe (Monster) Hurricane, for his insights into applied language aspect of the Russian language.

A special thanks to Daniel Pendleton, for all things art and computer science related: web platform; cover graphics and fonts; and hacking CMYK in Illustrator.

For:
Colonel Edwin (Ed) Motyka, USAF (Ret.)
Colonel Richard (Dick) Bukner, USA (Ret.)
William (Bill) Dukstein, DIA (RIP)
and
their insistence I join DIA

CONTENTS

CHAPTER ONE
Motoscafi

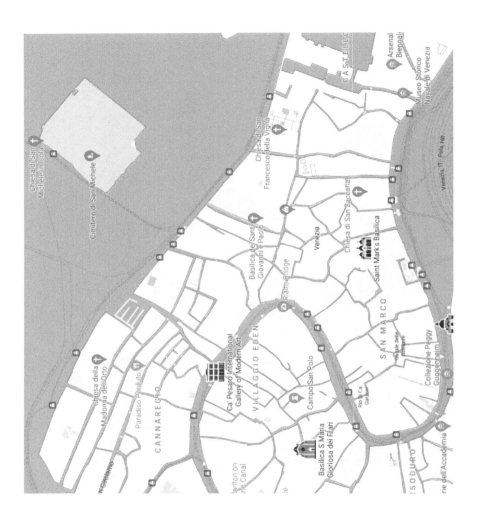

Motoscafi

Venice at night takes on an intimate, languid pace, releasing its frantic tension from the noontime frenzy of tourists under the blazing July sun, and hiding its pervasive litter and detritus in dim recesses and behind the shadowed corners of ornate gothic *palazzi*. The muted, warm lighting twinkles in the ripples of the Grand Canal, mere echoes of the bustling *vaporetti* and *gondole*, most of which now garaged themselves in slips or alongside docks. The warm glow reflects from the pastel-hued facades up into the night sky and, tonight, is cast back down, off a leaden ceiling of clouds low over the lagoon.

Flocks of tourists gravitate to the hundreds upon hundreds of restaurants like lovers meeting in tryst for the first time, dining in animated gaiety with voracious appetites for the romantic atmosphere and unique local cuisine. The scene repeats in each eatery, one of pulsing dinner parties, with loud murmurous conversations competing with the ringing of glasses in toast, the metallic din of forks on delicate porcelain, and the punctuation of popping corks. An occasional hearty bellow of regale serves to heighten the mood in an ever-rising tempo.

I alternated my attention between the floodlit white arch of the Ponte di Rialto ninety feet to my front, across the water; avoiding distraction from the complex flavors of Baccala Monecato on the white linen; my fellow Case Officer candidate, Monica Brigetti, watching my face; and trying to identify any supplemental countersurveillance teams which might lurk in the area.

"What are they doing?" she asked, over a bite of her sumptuous Bigoli pasta.

"They're ordering dessert, or espresso," I replied, glancing along the line of diners to a table thirty feet away.

"Either way, we'd better get moving," checking her antique Piaget.

We sat at the canal-side Terraza Sommariva surveilling two other CO candidates roleplaying as KGB officers conducting their SDR. They'd used four modes of countersurveillance thus far, and we expected they'd employ two or three more on their way to whatever tryst *they* were heading to tonight.

Dining-in at the same time they did was one of several effective means of covering them, but we'd need to depart before they did to remain non-suspicious. We'd confirmed they weren't running with a CS support team until now, although trailing trained HUMINT officers in Venice—remaining undetected—was arduous enough.

"Indeed," as I signaled to our *cameriere* for the bill. "But I wanted time for some Bacoli and Zabaglione," feigning a pout at her.

"At least I got you a side of Fritole. They'll have to do." So I popped one of the sugar-dusted pastry balls in my mouth as the waiter receded. Delicate… fantastic.

And discretely checked our pair of faux Ivans in the oblique-angle reflection off the Terraza's windows. Our prey's CS techniques were good, casually checking their environs periodically. Then again, we were all deep into SDR and CS training of the basic CO course, so you'd figure they'd learned a bit by now, at least how to walk and chew gum at the same time; they hadn't yet been murder-boarded out.

Monica and I agreed I'd keep a bead on the *kroliki* if they stopped in a lit area. My face was nondescript compared to hers. Although we both wore disguises, it was nearly impossible for her to cover up her pedigreed beauty. "You're not ugly enough for this business," I always taunted her when it came to remaining inconspicuous. Personally, I thought she was most likely tagged for work on the high-level diplomatic circuit where her asset against the opposite gender—weak and melting—would go far.

She dealt with the waiter as I kept tabs on our targets. They'd done a good job at their own disguises, dirtying themselves up to look like Russian *apparatchiki*. I finished my Baccala with a last sip of the Prosecco—*not too much, Ben, we're on the job*. Although I knew it'd take much more than the stingy amount I'd imbibed to cut through all the adrenaline I had running.

We slipped out of the terrace holding hands, down the Riva d'Vin, and moved out of the warm lighting and raucous atmosphere into shadow.

"You'll loop up?" she asked, to confirm.

"I'm on it," as we ducked into the shadowed tunnel of Calle di

Storione.

I strode deeper into the darkness of the side street, hurrying but not so fast as to attract attention, even though no one was in the vicinity. No street lamps, just the dim, hazy reflection off the low cloud cover to help me distinguish one shade of black from the next. Vivaldi's notes quickly faded in my wake. I also dared not hurry because of the footing here; the huge paving stones fit together tightly and smoothly, until you came upon an errant one standing proud and it ambushed your big toe. A spastic accident isn't supposed to be part of clandestine surveillance.

A few hundred feet, one zigzag, and I turned right onto the Ruga Vecchia San Giovanni, back into a lit, peopled area busy with open bakeries and boutiques. I estimated I'd need two minutes for the several hundred feet to return back north of the terrace restaurant and position myself in the alcove across from the base of the Ponte di Rialto. Two *very* long minutes, because our targets could decide to move on without a single sip of espresso, and if they moved east, I wouldn't be in position of coverage yet.

Right onto Ruga dei Oresi, more shops, past the Saint Giacomo church and the imposing Camerlenghi Palace—WWII bullet pockmarks and all—and slip into the alcove, trying not to breathe too hard.

Double-check. Where were our subjects?

I wondered about this training iteration, one of the few conducted overseas in real-world environs. The exercise was a GO / NO GO proposition: either you succeeded and might graduate, or didn't and, at best, would get sent to do desk work until you could plead your way back into a CO course. It made sense; partial credit doesn't exist out in the field... 'Excuse me, Mister GRU, don't I get at least a B for full effort?' Nevermind. Except presumably, our KGB role-players were operating under the same guidelines. Dog-eat-dog, and all that.

C'mon, Ben. Disregard. Focus on the targets.

Yeah, except the do-or-die GO / NO GO added just a touch of stress. Well, enough to keep the adrenaline jacked, for which I was thankful.

There they were. Only sixty feet distant and close enough to ascertain how *they* weren't passing up on the Zabaglione. Bastards.

I cycled two clicks into my comms gear to signal Monica I

was in place. If I had nothing else to tell her, it simply meant the targets were still in the box. It appeared they'd stay another five minutes, or even a half-hour, depending on whether they also ordered coffee.

Until it became apparent their countersurveillance moves were increasing, scanning actively, as if preparing to leave. I'd be required to report this in the AAR—After Action Review—and it wouldn't go well for them. Never show any indication you're conducting CS.

They were paying the bill.

We'd been surveilling them for over two hours, from the church on the island of San Michele, when the day had been bright and sunny with long shadows to all the gravestones, following them in their complicated gyrations all the way here. Their SDR would last another two hours, at least.

They'd motored away from a dock by the 500-year-old church in a *motoscafo,* and we'd needed to scramble to our own powerboat. Which was stashed under the lee of a pier on the far side of the small square island. Still, it was a couple hundred yards over the stone walls, around crypts, and through rows of gravestones. The graves of Igor Stravinsky and Ezra Pound were around here somewhere, but no time to stop for any genealogy. At least we'd tagged our targets' boat with a micro-miniature tracker—well, Monica had, while I kept track of them. It was a simple time-pulsed signal which hid within the electromagnetic noise of the engine's ignition system, but our GPS receiver side-linked to a Differential GPS transmitter the Agency had set up in Venice gave us their location to within a few inches.

We tracked their southerly progress as we ripped along to the southeast. The target box was the historic city, so Monica and I began with the assumption—*careful*—they'd head south or west.

"Okay, they're moving south rather than west now," Monica declared.

"Just don't try to spot them." They were over a half-mile distant, but the bearing to them was smack in the middle of a vast blotch of intense silver reflection off the lagoon's waters. We'd appear vivid to them in their countersurveillance.

"I'd make their heading as due south," she said. "Any thoughts of where they're headed?"

Beta

I worked to recall the northern shore's topography from my exhaustive studies back at Langley.

"I'd disappear into the city at this point, not just find a docking spot along the Fondamente." I wracked my brain as she steered. "I'd put them at the Rio Mendicanti or Rio di Santa Glustina," I thought out loud. "Perhaps the Rio del Gesulti…"

"I concur," as she squinted at the westering sun. "I'm going to starting curving south."

I knew she saw in her mind exactly what I did, from her own studies. She and I clicked rather well, despite the age disparity.

"We'll need to go in parallel," I added, "and use San Marina or Giovanni Laterano to stay on their track."

"Roger."

We were like any other *motoscafo* out here among the dozens and would appear just as we intended, skating over the mild waves at thirty knots, except away from our quarry—ostensibly.

As we continued curving south, the wind buffeted over our heads behind the windscreen, and the situation changed.

"Okay, we're in front of them now, regarding the north-south bearing."

"Perfect, Ben. I always love following from in front," her patent smile of mischievous joy taking over.

"Wait one… wait one," monitoring the GPS tracker. "The range is decreasing slightly… steadily."

"They're east of south, heading for Santa Glustina?"

"Possibly," I mulled it over for a second. Then, "We'll have to parallel them via the Galeazze channel."

"Where the hell's?—Oh, yeah. Okay. I got it."

"What are the odds they'll take it all the way to San Marco channel?"

"Too easy, Ben. They'll be stuck in a single-lane canal all the way. Too constricting."

"Yeah, you're right," which she was. It was a decent chokepoint, but almost a half-mile long. Still, the dense boat traffic of the San Marco channel would be attractive, even without room to maneuver. *Shit, Ben. Chill out.* Just let things unfold, feeling somewhat green.

"I think I can see them," Monica commented, the viewing angle no longer directly into Sol.

"Okay, but nothing more than a quick glance. One of them may be using binoculars."

"Right you are, Ben." One of the great advantages of working in tandem was having two brains operating together, even pinging each other to higher perceptions and insights, one-plus-one quite a bit more than two. But only when the two operators mesh well.

I sank down in the left seat, Monica's silhouette blocking my body from a northwest vector, and peeked an eye around the nape of her neck. We were on a heading toward Bacini, well distant from our targets.

"Okay, they're definitely headed toward Santa Gristina," I concluded.

"Or they could still pull up to the north shore. Hell, they might return the boat to the rental service by the hospital."

In other words: stop leaping to assumptions. Touché.

"Roger that," once again, realizing my anxiousness.

"But keep peeking…"

Even so, I needed to keep a running tally of all the possible tactical scenarios that could unfold and work out our own moves before the fact, so we could react seamlessly.

"Alright. Let's make for Bacini and dock. Exit fully from their CS envelope and see what happens." This was extremely risky for maintaining surveillance, but we had nothing better.

"Yeah, they're not gonna' dock," Monica concluded.

Right. Until they did. And switched back to foot mode. Then we'd lose them.

"I agree. It doesn't feel like they're ready to switch yet. Too soon." We were both experiencing the same mission-feel. Or perhaps we were feeding off each other. Regardless, we might still be wrong.

We came down off plane, with the buffeting wind receding and a shove from our own wake as Monica cut the throttle at once, turned, and glided gently behind a small jetty housing a few other *motoscafi*. She was more than smooth, handling the heavy wooden craft deftly.

C'mon, Ben, don't start with the imagination again.

The late afternoon blaze from the beating sun returned. Small waves lapped at the shore wall, and dozens of foraging gulls wheeled under the broken clouds.

As our targets idled into the Rio di Santa Giustina.

I breathed again.

"They could reverse and pop back out," I voiced, an effective CS move.

"Keep an eye on the GPS, Ben."

"Got them."

"Yeah, either way, we need to move," and she pulled back out, the exhaust from the inboard burbling behind us as a lone gull atop a piling swiveled its head to inspect us. We needed a programmable gull with camera strapped to it, I thought. Stay right on them.

Shut up, Ben. No time for entertainment.

"Okay. So we parallel them along the Galeazze channel. Better move it."

And she slammed the throttle to its stop, sitting me back down in my seat with a slap. The channel entrance was a quarter-mile ahead, somewhere in the glare of sun spreading out before us.

We reached the entrance, slowed, entered, and transited the channel into the Arsenale boathouse section, the 120-foot wide waterway allowing for decent headway. The GPS was tracking them tightly.

"Uh oh. Range is moving a lot now. They're slipping behind us," I reported.

"Got it. I'll turn into Rio Gorne," picking our way around several ambling four-meter outboards.

"Wait one. Wait..." a few more seconds. "They're moving south again."

"Must have jogged over to the San Lorenzo," she thought out loud.

"Yep, think you're right," I echoed. "All ahead one-third, cap'n."

She threw me an excited stare. We were both getting into it now, having *not* lost them. But, of course, one of the two might have debarked, or they may have executed a complete switch. This was no way to run a railroad, I thought: you'd need a platoon for mobile surveillance inside Venice's maze, or an entire battalion to set up static posts.

We passed under a stout wooden bridge and between the twin towers of the Arsenale, the lions, statues, and a gryphon off to the right. The Purgatory bridge farther back—some kind of tribute to Dante. *Disregard, Ben.* And back into a more populated area. We needed to slow to a sedate speed in this narrow canal.

"They're still behind us. We should be able to get out into San Marco to see them emerge."

"Keep an eye on that thing," she ordered. "There are still several places they could turn."

"Got it." The GPS readout progressed steadily.

"We'd better do hats," I announced.

Time for another appearance change. At least we didn't need to worry about the appearance of our *motoscafo*; the rental versions all appeared the same.

We emerged under the stone brick of the Riva Biagio, one of several boats in the cramped line through the tight opening.

"How 'bout half-throttle toward the Grigio Maggiore?"

"Already on it," as she swung around the line and accelerated.

Water taxis, motorboats, even a cruise ship filled the San Marco channel, seeming to travel in every direction at once, yet in an uncharacteristic—for Italy—orderly fashion. Much better than the roads; perhaps drowning was a less attractive prospect than a fender bender.

I shrank down again in my seat to look past her neck, alternating views of the GPS display and the canal opening just the other side of one of the ferry terminals. A constant, sporadic stream of watercraft flowed from the Rio del Greci. Too many looked the same, and our targets may have changed appearance too. Hats stood out everywhere.

"Shit. They found a group of similar *motoscafi* to blend with," I groaned.

"Here, use the monocular," handing me the mini spotting scope.

I squinted and scanned, pausing at each boat in the distance. Tried the zoom.

Squinting didn't help, and the boats were fanning out in every direction.

"Their general direction is toward the inner city," Monica opined. "I'm going to turn west and parallel the Bacino. It should improve our ability to tail them."

We curved and slid within fifty feet of the basin packed with parked sailboats on the north side of the San Giorgio Maggiore Island and picked up speed to fifteen knots.

A minute passed. Getting anxious again. Then another minute. *Shit.*

"C'mon, Ben. What's going on?" She felt it, too.

"We're moving in the same direction as the targets."

"Okay. But spot 'em already," strident now.

"Can you pick up speed? Aim for the Punta?"

The ten-foot golden conch by the Palladian Church slid past to port. After a half-minute, the GPS showed movement.

"Got 'em. They're wearing ball caps now," I announced. "One white and one blue."

"You got them? You're sure?"

"Yes, it's the same registration number on the bow." Even though it wasn't entirely legible in the zoom of the monocular because of the range and motion of both boats.

"We'd better cross over," Monica announced, follow from in front again. "They might go on foot at any moment. I'd like Saint Mark's Square for CS this time of day."

They were out in the channel and looked to be reversing course.

"Wait one. They're doubling back."

Or looping in a circle. Clearing their baffles?

"They're headed back. Away from us."

"Okay. I'm going to angle toward the shore. We can hide among the extra traffic."

"Roger. Sounds good."

We motored perpendicular to the channel's traffic lanes and bouncing with a lot of the chop from wakes.

"Nope, they're looping. Shit. I can't see them." A heavy wooden three-master, at least a hundred feet long, was transiting between us. "Get us on the other side of that POS sailboat."

"I'm on it," nudging the throttle.

"Shit. Where'd they go?" when we passed the sailor. I hunted around like crazy, sunken in the seat and behind Monica.

"Okay. Okay. Yep, got 'em. They're angling toward the shore. They're at your two o'clock, white and blue caps still." We were within a couple hundred yards by now. It was becoming nerve-wracking.

"Shit, Ben, they're close. We need to do better." We were out in the open, exposed, so she swung the helm to port, away.

I wasn't prepared for the move and tipped off my seat, landing between us. And with my head tight in her lap. *Oops.*

"No time for that now, Ben," off-handed.

Hell, she was cool. Nothing phased her.

We both laughed. It was more than incongruous at the moment. "Shit. Sorry," scrambling back into the white leather on my side as we continued the turn, dodging other travelers. Yeah, her sense of humor definitely had roots in the military. I'd pegged her as an Air Force officer, a Lieutenant Colonel, two nights ago, back at Peary as we planned this jaunt. I'd blown her training cover.

C'mon, Ben, back to the present. More about that later.

We were traveling east, opposite our quarry. Now over 200 yards distant.

"They're angling toward the San Marco ferry terminal," I reported. "Heading to shore. Possibly transitioning to foot mode."

"Got it." She was processing silently and making course corrections. I kept the monocular on them, but tried to figure out what they were thinking, and what Monica was thinking.

"What, you thinking they'll debark, then reverse toward Saint Mark's?" I asked.

"Perhaps," but she was making her own play, turning toward shore and angling to the east end of the Doge's Palace. If our targets were intent on Saint Mark's, we'd be ahead of them again.

This was a high-risk gamble, I thought. We'd be over a hundred yards from them and probably lose them if they proceeded west. What if they headed into the old Royal Gardens? It was commercial now, open.

"Uh, Monica?"

"What?" Jockeying us around and through the haphazard shore traffic, including a couple of rude gestures: how she was driving like a *Parisienne.*

"If they use the old Royal Gardens, we may be fucked." I'd studied it as a viable CS location but had forgotten most of its details. Did it have side or rear exits?

Crap.

"Yeah. They could use it as a chokepoint but may either

reverse or transit through. Except they'd have to get over a canal with no bridge." She swung us close to the Ponte della Paglia for a double-park maneuver with a similar *motoscafo* tied to the dock. "Catch that boat and tie up the rear. I'll get the front," as she reversed the propeller for two seconds to stop us a half-foot from it, then killed the engine.

She'd jogged my memory, though, "Yeah, or they might hop on a *gondola* and come back out. Around it. On the other side." I cursed how this exercise had been set up: using a GPS tracker for exact location, but only a two-person team for surveillance. Sure, the environment around the targets would be much less dirty—no platoon of countersurveillants to be sensed—but there were too many permutations the faux Ivans might utilize. It struck me then: this experimental method needed at least two teams, one in front and one trailing. Or maybe that's what Monica and I were supposed to have figured out at the outset... we had comms after all.

Shit. Maybe they intended to fail us.

Or just me.

Beta

CHAPTER TWO
San Marco

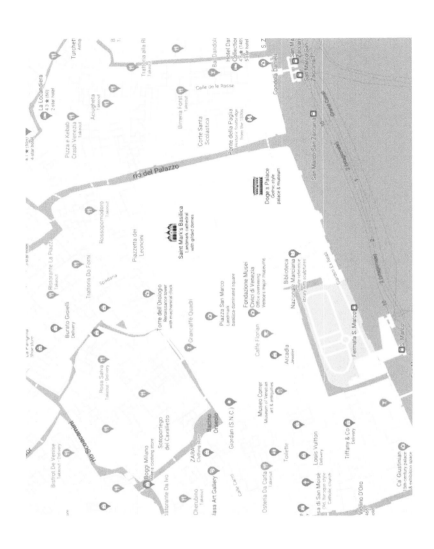

San Marco

"Let's get to the top of the bridge," she squawked, no longer implacable.

The broad thoroughfare along the shore was crammed with people and rife with kiosks, hawking everything from t-shirts and sunhats to paintings and marionettes. No time for souvenirs or party tricks, though, because a packed and milling tour group was making its way up the bridge, crowding everyone else out.

"*Scusami.* Scusami." Monica chirped, trying to get us past them in her fluent Italian.

"I say, what's that bird all about?" came back in twangy cockney.

She was more tailback than fullback, deftly weaving her way around and through the defensive throng. I turned sideways and tried to keep up.

At the bridge's top—the only vantage point for hundreds of yards—she snatched the monocular from my grasp, crouched behind the stone railing, and peered up along the busy shoreline. I stood behind her, shielding her from the infinite bumps and jostles she'd otherwise suffer from the oblivious tourists. Yes, we learn even these sorts of details in training.

I had no way of finding our targets in all the bustle at this range, and Monica was exercising her prerogative as the team leader, snatching the stubby telescope from me. Her anxiousness outpaced my own by now. We'd been substantially closer to shore than our targets when we'd tied up, so they should still be visible.

C'mon, Moni. Find them.

"*Merda,*" she hissed.

I felt graduation slipping from my grasp.

"Nope. Got 'em," she announced.

Surveillance isn't supposed to be emotionally tiring, except there's always something dire at stake.

"They're tying up. They're still wearing those silly hats."

"Which reminds me," I answered. "We need to remove ours." Change appearance when you change travel modes.

"Right. Thanks."

"You cover them in the Gardens if they use them. I'll cover the Rio from Harry's Bar. Let me know." She meant to let her know if they returned to the boat and headed back into the main channel.

"Roger. And if they come toward us, we split. You go ninety,"—degrees—"and stop. I'll continue on."

We proceeded through the gauntlet of self-absorbed pedestrians: tourists lugging ten-pound cameras; late afternoon tipplers catching their balance on the way to their next glass; map-toting pedestrians lost in the paper in front of them, bumping everyone; and over-animated girlfriends shrieking over the latest chintz they'd bought. The entire Riva was a surveillance nightmare. The swirling masses provided mobile concealment in every direction, and the tourist kiosks formed a chaotic labyrinth of choke points, hides, and reverse opportunities.

Monica stayed to the outside, moving gracefully from mobile cover to mobile cover. At the same time, I slid along the line of buildings in a half-hunched walk through the elusive gaps between shuffling people.

Where were they?

I keyed my whisper mic, trying to speak like a ventriloquist. "Anything?" She had a better angle on the pedestrian cross-section.

"Wait one. I'm isolating the hats." Standard, if they hadn't doffed them…

I kept moving, over a raised wooden ramp-way and into the area in front of the Gardens, more kiosks being swarmed. The 400-foot long garden fence stretched out in front of me behind the row of kiosks.

This was it. Do or die. It was time.

"Monica?" I keyed.

"They split up. They're halfway along the Gardens. Missus White's at a kiosk. Professor Plum is by the shore railing. They're scanning. Looking for surveillance. Us."

"Roger." *Thank God.*

"You see me?"

"No, I'm near the end."

"Okay. I'm gonna' pass through." I took out my own tourist map and worked to become self-absorbed, another boob tourist. Monica had them covered for the moment.

After a moment of ambling, "They're moving."

"Which way?" I asked.

Pause. I waited. Stopped to check a bauble. I'd not yet reacquired the targets myself.

Another two seconds... *two hours*.

The muted squelch broke in my ear, giving a jolt to my surging adrenaline.

"That's it. The Gardens."

"I'm moving," and looped around the shopping crowds, along the haphazard line of sidewalk trees toward the midpoint of the Gardens. There was just a single entrance on this side.

Shit. A pair of dark blue uniforms with sunglasses and pistol belts were head-on to my front. *Slow down, Ben.* There weren't supposed to be any CS teams, but I could still get detained and be ticketed if I ran over a pair of cops. Our eyes met, then I shifted mine to the left, over one's shoulder, and feigned surprised recognition of finding my lost companion—'oh, there you are, honey,' and swerved to the left toward the shore railing.

It happens.

After a moment at the stone railing next to a female stranger, I glanced around. All clear.

Then made a smooth beeline to the entrance of the Royal Gardens.

No sign of the targets.

"I'm going in," I whispered.

A single click.

The historic Royal Gardens were multi-hued shades of green, vivid in the late afternoon shadows after having suffered the glare of the lagoon. Soon the shadows would turn to twilight, transforming the alleyed city into a labyrinth of canyons and tunnels. I was going in to find our Ivans and track them, track their moves within this eden-like chokepoint. Which also meant they'd see me—or could, at least. I made a mental bookmark of my disguise at this point: map in hand; distracted; erect posture and upright gait; light blue windbreaker. I'd need to drastically change appearance after covering them in here and not use this one again.

A single paved-gravel path looped around inside the perimeter of the Gardens, lined with benches, pedestal planters, and a haphazard variety of bushes, ivies, and dwarf trees. The greenspace attracted starry-eyed couples more than it did hungry tourists.

White and Plum—they still hadn't removed their headgear—may have gone left, right, or split up. I was hiding in plain sight, making myself conspicuous—to be less so. I adopted my best gawping-eyed tourist demeanor.

Where the hell were they?

My loop to the left—the shorter leg—led to the Rio along the north side with a few *gondole* awaiting fares and several lovers spaced out along the path. I wasn't alone—good—but I was the only single person. If they took note of me, would my lack of a camera be remarkable? There was nothing I could do about it.

There they were. At a range of over 200 feet, gesturing like locals in conversation and casually looking everywhere. Fairly obvious to the initiated.

"Got 'em," I whispered.

Another click in return.

I did my best to refer to my map, the variegated fauna all around, and make myself conspicuous. Yet oblivious to those around me.

This was the tense part. I was in range of the enemy and might get blown. I used my peripheral vision to monitor them, their general shapes and colors, enough to keep tabs. I checked a mounted info plaque to my front, describing the *tilia cordata* I was so engrossed in.

Would they start to move, or were they dawdling, to flush out tags?

I needed to keep moving at a steady pace. Keep up the role camouflage as a nature geek. *Shit*, right under their noses. I took out a small pad and a pen and started taking notes. Oooh… *hedera canariensis.*

They were taking the patient approach, looking for anyone out of place. I knew I was obvious—perhaps too obvious—but later on, they'd encounter nothing resembling my current persona.

They disappeared around the far loop as I approached the one to the east.

"They may be making for the entrance. They didn't hire a *gondola*," I let Monica know.

"Watch out for a second circuit." She knew what sort of cover I'd adopted and warned me to maintain it.

"Roger. But you'd better cover the entrance."

"Already moving."

I breathed a sigh and relaxed an iota. I *did not* want to lose them again. I kept up my arboreal education but crept my way back around to the front path.

Another two minutes, a lifetime.

We'd agreed I'd go after them if a chance existed they'd notice one of us. Monica was just too striking with her northern Mediterranean bone structure and stately height; even with appearance changes, there'd be a risk of catching her as a repeat if the chase went on long enough.

"I got 'em. They're exiting. No hats. Dark green and blue tops now."

Excellent. We'd kept them in the box.

"On my way. I'm morphing too," I chimed.

The intricate environs were advantageous for an appearance change. I quickly stored my map and pad, reversed my windbreaker—dark blue now—pulled out a pair of dark horn-rimmed glasses, and shrunk my posture and gait.

Monica startled me as I emerged, did a double-take until she recognized my transformation, and then pointed her chin in the general direction of our Ivans. She'd put on large-framed rose-tinted glasses with a white windbreaker; still impossible not to know it was her.

There they were.

Yeah, back in the box. Except hardly a box; there were just the two of us.

What followed was more of a standard, lower risk tagging operation, using the large churning crowds as mobile cover as we split up and 'followed without following.'

"Bet they're headed to San Marco," she predicted.

"I won't take that bet."

"You want the near side or far side?" she asked.

"Near. You glide through these masses much better than me."

"Roger."

We ended up tracking them over the large herringbone street blocks and white stones in hopscotch patterns, up into Saint Mark's Square. Keeping into the shadows of the buildings to each side of the 120-foot wide entry *piazetta*.

The Piazza itself was a mobbed sea of raucous humanity; snippets of a dozen languages assaulted the ears as the Doge's Palace gave way to the three-hundred-year-old Basilica of San Marco, and its volumes of western byzantine architectural history. Domed, ornate, gilded, frescoed, gargoyled, columned, rose-paned... you name it.

No time for sightseeing, though, because the packed, roiling crowds made it a bitch to keep the targets in sight.

"I think they're zigzagging," I tried. Yeah, I would have programmed this square in my own SDR, especially for this time of day.

"Okay. I'll head into the center." She could conceivably maintain target lock that way without following their gyrations.

"Good idea. What are the odds they'll use one of the north-side tunnels?" I pondered out loud.

"A chokepoint like that after an open area is right out of the manual. So, yeah, but we still need to maintain lock."

Yeah, sure. They'll go by the manual. Until they don't.

"They're moving through 6:2, general direction toward 1:1," she reported. A handful of large open spaces dotted Venice proper; we'd made sure to grid-sect them during our prep. Standard, and not a waste of time, especially in this roiling, kaleidoscopic sea of colored tops and hats.

"Copy. They're going for Cavelletto or Salvadago, I bet."

I wracked my brain, stretching the adrenaline and B-12 megadoses to their max. I knew the ones she was referring to, but not which—not which tunnel was which.

I remembered the layout. If our quarry took the farther one, they could be executing a rapid direction change to flush us; it contained a 110-degree turn that dove into the dark alleys of the greater San Marco district.

"Moni, if they take the farther tunnel, it might be a rabbit move to flush us. Can you get ahead of them, down that one?"

"Or they might split up, use both, and join back up in five or ten minutes. Either way, yeah, I'm going for Salvadago." Aha, that's the farther one.

"They're at 4:3. I'll take the other tunnel. Cavelletto."

"I see them."

"Still together."

I veered thirty degrees to the right, directly toward the streaked white gothic facade of the prosecutor general's offices. The outer verges of the square were filled with clustered groups of tourists, which made sighting the targets slightly less complicated.

"I'm into the Salvadago, thirty feet in, along the canal," she announced. That was quick.

"Roger. I'm still trailing. I'll let you know..." which tunnel they used. Or if they doubled and remained in the square. I recalled details of the area into which they were headed: a tight, jumbled warren deep inside the district. Yeah, Monica decided on the best location, at the other end of the farthest tunnel, to either stay ahead of them if they followed the canal or fall in behind if they headed deeper into San Marco. She could direct me around them, to leapfrog in front.

Our Ivans were looking around, almost conspicuous in their CS technique, to me anyway—they must be from a class behind us, not over the hump yet, when the streets start to become intuitive. I stopped behind a tourist cluster and feigned reading the outdoor café's menu, resting on the brass standard of its velvet-roped barrier. Oooh... Gnocchi di Quattro Formaggio—four-cheese gnoc—and needed to wrench myself back to the present because my taste buds were out to take control—

And the targets moved. With purpose. In my direction.

Shit.

But no. Not looking at me.

"They're moving into Cavalletto," I reported.

"Copy."

So throw out Plan A and devise a Plan B. They headed into the shadowed recess of the building's tunnel, at once a pillared alcove between Olivetti and a small thermal power substation.

I trailed at fifty feet with my slumped-over, shuffling gait.

They accelerated their pace to observe whether anyone else did, as well.

"They're moving, speeding up," I quipped.

"Roger. I'm moving up to the next bridge to remain in front."

"We'd better alter our appearance again."

We did so.

What followed became a stop-action strobe of tenth-century images as I began leapfrogging ahead and behind the targets, trading quipped instructions with Monica, as we shadow-darted through the warren of tight alleys in the heart of thousand-year-old San Marco. The eight-foot-wide paths became dusk-filled crevasses of shops, theaters, hotels, and eateries, with muted orange auras casting glowing patches across the heavy stone walkways. We anticipated their moves—half the time correctly, half the time wrong—and maintained a running overwatch-and-move routine over tight canal bridges, through wafts of cooking crustaceans, chocolate aromas, and snippets of Rossini spilling into the late afternoon trundle of tired tourists.

Our faux KGB pair moved and stopped, moved and stopped, hopped in a *gondola*, then debarked 200 feet farther along. They looped around small open spaces and dove through churches. This is the intense heat of surveillance, driving the adrenaline and pulse to twitchy levels, making my breath ragged and threatening to cause a trip or stumble into one of the canals. Monica must be *enjoying* it too. I split my attention between partial memory of all the alleys, a high-res tourist map, maintaining natural pace and demeanor, and Monica's incessant squawking in my left ear. We changed appearances twice more, the minor details of maintaining surveillance. Oh, and the little thing about remaining invisible to our prey. My skin felt galvanized; my sight, hearing, and smell heightened. Time dilated, and I moved into the zone, the zone of becoming one with the environment and a master of smooth movement. Monica was even better, despite her striking, memorable visage. They *would not* get away.

Or flush us.

We stayed with them like a pair of invisible remoras attached to wary sharks.

CHAPTER THREE
Shadows

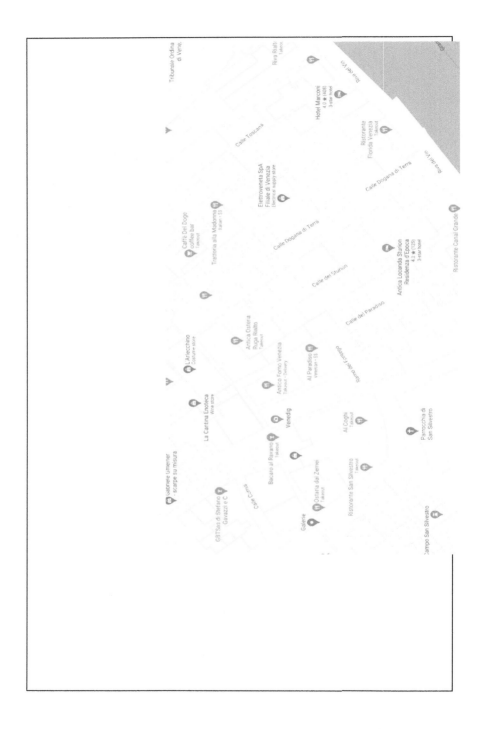

Shadows

Until they returned to the boardwalk of the Grand Canal and hired another gondola, this time taking a lazy tour up the canal amidst the glut of motoring water traffic.

Monica and I rendezvoused by Harry's in time to observe their departure and change of appearance. The frantic stop-action of their movements came to halt like a car slamming into a bridge abutment, killing our urgency and leaving us as a pair of over-revving Ferraris in neutral. They'd become Missus White and Professor Plum again.

Monica looked like the cross between an alien and a chipmunk, with the huge round sunglasses framed under a fur kepi. I stifled a laugh, a bit more concerned about the imminent loss of our quarry.

"Vaporetto," she blurted, as she brushed past me, out onto the pier of a ferry terminal.

Yeah, good thinking, as I read her mind about our next surveillance mode. Something faster than their *gondola*, catch up and follow from in front again. We couldn't simply jump in a *gondola* ourselves… 'Follow that *gondola*,' doesn't work in real life.

Our water taxi would motor past the Ivans, and we'd remain concealed in the boat's crowd. The fifteen-meter taxis stop at terminals every quarter- to half-mile. We could pick and choose our next stops, our next moves. At least, that's what I hoped Moni was thinking.

Hope is a killer in our trade.

"Let's separate," she ordered. "You sit in the bow. I'll move aft," as she removed her alien face.

"Sure. Good idea."

The *vaporetto* was a packed sardine tin, rolling in the multiple wakes caused by the other large craft churning about the Grand Canal. The water taxi was filled with a quiet din of half-a-dozen foreign languages and fingers pointing in delight in every direction. We headed out into the narrowing thoroughfare into the setting sun's glare. Sitting near the bow, I was responsible for reestablishing target-lock again, but my glare-burned retinae were having none of it.

"I can't see shit."

"Copy."

We were two or three minutes behind the stroke-propelled *gondola*. They might have pulled the on-and-off maneuver again, but it would be inconsistent with tradecraft protocols: vary, vary, and vary. Repeating a move becomes dangerous all too fast.

Still, tension flooded me, and I squinted with pain and welling tears, scanning left-right, right-left to pick up whatever off-center images I could.

No go. The tears just blurred everything. I needed to cover my eyes and give them a chance to recover.

We were overtaking the slower *gondole* as they trundled along the canal's side.

"Tell me you've got them," Monica implored.

"Wait one. We're overtaking several *gondole*." I didn't think it would reassure her to tell her I was *permanently* blind.

Shit.

This could result in the NO GO grade real quick. She'd wouldn't appreciate that, either.

"C'mon, Ben."

"Just a sec." I tried hope, denial, prayer to Saint Joshua, and futile despair. Nothing worked; I was asking for a clandestine miracle.

A blue hat and a white hat, sliding aft on our starboard beam at fifty feet. Within a cluster of the meandering *gondole*.

Double-check. *Stay casual, Ben.*

"Got 'em."

"Thank God."

Fifty feet off the beam, inside a cluster of *gondole*, sliding aft.

"Left or right?"

"Sorry. Right."

The span of a heartbeat.

"Yes. That's them," I heard from her.

Thank God, I thought, too. I might have been mistaken, and the number of times Murphy trumps Saint Joshua in this business is incalculable. A rigid stiffness of tension along my entire body relaxed. Another reprieve.

Beta

For now.

We kept them in the bubble at the first stop, but outstripped them by the second one—by the Ponte dell' Accademia—and needed to debark. We watched from a shadowed recess between two buildings as they sailed up the canal, creeping past. Moni held me in a loose embrace, in case anyone observed us. "No time for this now, Monica." And we both laughed, just like the young lovers we pretended to be.

We picked up the next *vaporetto* and repeated the move twice more. It was a surveillance technique we winged, on the fly. Hell, a tradecraft technique that may someday become a footnote in a manual addendum for future classes. We felt confident and in control again.

"Careful. They might be trying to lull us," I suggested. One of my own favorite ploys.

"Yeah, right. They've been at this a half-hour. We need to expect they'll move any second."

"Roger. They could stop anywhere in a *gondola*. Then fade." We were thinking ahead by only a single minute now. Yeah, lulled.

No longer confident and in control.

Under the Ponte di Rialto and around the second curve of the Grand Canal's 'S,' with my adrenaline spiking again.

Think, Ben. Think.

"I'm debarking at the next terminal," I instructed. "You stay on. I'll pick up a *vaporetto* if they keep moving."

"Roger. I'll debark at the subsequent stop, and we can switch to motor-*gondole*, leapfrogging each other if they continue." She didn't mind my giving her an order despite her senior rank; position in the food chain doesn't enter into high-pucker-factor clandestine ops.

I debarked and took up surveillance along the Fondamenta Vin Castello, changing appearance for the umpteenth time and using concealment within the stalls of the fish market. Our prey floated past, creeping along to the oscillations of the gondolier.

Lull us? Shit, they were about to bore me to death.

Indeed. These ops transition from panic to sleep and back again. Too many times.

"I'm at the House of Gold. Waiting," she announced.

"Roger. You should be able to reacquire them. They're about

200 feet from your pos."

"Copy."

I kept pace on foot, fifty feet to their rear, set back inside the market's stalls. They reeked of whitefish and crustaceans, pungent and oily.

"They're debarking at the Rio Beccarie," she announced.

"I'm moving." Only in a half-panic, because I could pick them up by taking a parallel alleyway which came out at the first bridge over the *rio*.

Except, "I'm gonna' need you on this side *ASAP*, Moni."

"Ya' think?" she retorted. Yeah, still the boss. "I'm picking up a taxi this minute," she added.

"Thanks."

Our pair of 'KGB agents' walked towards me along the *rio's* alley. I receded from the bridge I was using, my back to them. I could cover them on another parallel route, sighting through the covered stalls of the Beccarie market. But Monica had better arrive soon, or I'd need to cover them up close, risk blowing myself.

They turned inward, entering into the covered market. Toward me, again.

Closing.

I continued on, perpendicular to them. Hiding inside the stalls and the sea of people until I felt safe enough to turn around and reacquire.

"I'm here," in my left ear.

Thank God.

"They're futzing around inside the market a hundred feet down the *rio*," I replied.

What followed was a repeat version of the cat-and-mouse gyrations we'd performed in San Marco's labyrinth. This time in San Polo, except their gyrations lasted a mere ten minutes until they doubled back, settling in at the Terrazza Sommariva.

We could breathe again. For a few minutes.

* * *

Until now, with the adrenaline pulsing and the blood singing in my ears as I homed in on their track again. No hats anymore, and dressed in dark hues, befitting the dusk, as it died toward night.

They moved off, down toward Monica, and my brain jumped ahead two beats—they had three options: hop in a *gondola*; take the tunnel Moni was in; or use one of the other four tunnel alleys away from the Riva del Vin.

"Moving your way," I whispered, picking up the pace along the Riva. She had to rely on my reporting their movements since she was hidden, and would now be retreating down the Calle Dogana in case they turned into it. Yeah, follow from ahead, better than having them run over you.

I moved through the sitting crowds of insatiable revelers, oblivious and drowning in a haze of red wine and overloaded taste buds. The energetic notes of Vivaldi and an endless medley of succulent aromas distracted me, trying to pull me back into their clutches.

I moved away from their temptations, locked onto the back of the necks of my Ivans, and kept pace, a hundred feet back and seeing nothing but them.

Careful, Ben. Watch out for target-lock obsession, and keep an eye on the obstacles. No tripping into the canal.

"Approaching your position," I reported.

"Copy. I'm back a hundred feet."

"They're not turning."

"Okay. Either a *gondola* or one of the other alleys," she thought out loud.

"There's a *vaporetto* terminal at the end of the Riva. Or they might fade into the last alley, double around, and return to the terminal."

Oh, joy. Nothing like optimistic, happy thoughts.

"I'm on my way," immediately recognizing how I'd just described the worst-case scenario. One of the most effective techniques in countersurveillance is to radically alter speed as you disappear around corners, and make random turns at unpredictable moments.

I wondered if our prey were smart enough to have memorized the water-bus schedules, then discarded the notion, schedules being one more thing for the independent-minded Italians to scoff at. Regardless, if they hopped a *vaporetto,* we couldn't embark with them, and the next one wouldn't arrive for another five or ten minutes. And any other *gondola* certainly wouldn't be able to catch up.

"I think it's okay," I tried. "There's bound to be a couple of *motoscafi* along the Riva, if we need."

"Or steal," hearing her winded suggestion as she ran to catch up. Too much Rigoli...

"Ummm..."

Late dusk along the Grand Canal shined like a serpentine necklace of gold, the banks of warm orange lighting reflecting off the undulating waters and casting a pulsing glow on the facades of the stoic buildings presiding over the scene.

No time for sightseeing, Ben.

Our Ivans weaved in and out of the sparse crowds over a hundred feet ahead. Tracking them became sketchy; I'd better pick up the pace. I moved with the crowd's ebb and flow, using them as mobile concealment. No weaving and dodging for me, then the image of them dining flashed back in my mind. They hadn't faked drinking, and each had imbibed three vodkas and two glasses of wine. So our fellow trainees were fully in role. Still, that much alcohol was a mistake in tradecraft. Just wait until the AAR, I thought.

Disregard, as I was elbowed from the right and half-stumbled. I checked up and—

"Where are they?" Monica whispered, hooking her arm inside my elbow. I didn't mind our role camouflage as a romantic couple, but needed to make sure her magnetic distraction didn't overcome me.

"They're approaching the end of the last restaurant."

"Where? Oh, okay. I got 'em."

They turned into San Silvestro, an open, wide alley near the Riva's end. I wracked my memory to recall the network of alleys in the area. Shit. I already should have the image in my head. The surveillance started to drag on me—*after only three hours.* Attribute it to the challenge of Venice itself; but *crap,* it didn't help.

"Jump ahead to the last alley, into the Capo San Silvestro. Try to pass them. I'll trail." Monica *had* recalled the exact layout, saving me.

"Roger." I could only agree, as I sped up and struggled to

retrieve the overhead image of the warren of alleys in my mind.

They kept on straight when the San Silvestro turned left, Monica reported. They were transitioning from a broad, well-lit alley into a narrow, dark strip.

"You'd better stay on Silvestro," I chirped, knowing that when they slipped into the dark, they'd stop and observe behind themselves for any trailers.

"Roger. You jump ahead," she came back. I'd only told her the obvious, but it wouldn't insult; it's the reason we're teamed in pairs. And check your ego at the door.

The overhead sat image of the labyrinth we worked now coalesced. Adrenaline jolted me after almost losing my sanity back there and returned me to focus. The alley they'd entered continued ahead a hundred yards into a dead-end, yet with two intersections along the way. I didn't think their ultimate goal was in its terminus; it was too early for them to complete their SDR, slightly over three hours by now. I could keep them in sight in the gloom at something like fifty feet.

We assumed they'd pause to check their rear from inside a dark recess, which was a safe assumption. Except the nerves started conjuring all sorts of yelling and spitting in my face during the After Action Review, if I lost them.

"You'd better take the L'Ogio ode la Rugleta," Monica scolded. Never pass up the opportunity to bust on your partner in this trade. But I knew she was on it.

I turned down the Calle Curnis, approaching the dead-end turnoff. The light in these unpopulated warrens fled, slammed shut. I reversed my light windbreaker, covering myself with a camouflage of midnight blue. I was slinking, gliding into the dead-end T-intersection, left, then immediately right, into a black-shadowed alley ten-feet deep and two stories high. I breathed a silent sigh as I took up position to view the T-intersection, down on my haunches and still as a deer waiting to drink. I gave Monica two clicks over comms, which she returned with one: acknowledged. She knew where I was headed and that I was now in position to observe. If our fake Soviet quarry didn't turn left or right into the Calle blah-blah-blah Rugheta, they'd pass right in front of me and turn left onto Calle Curnis. This was a critical juncture in our surveillance exercise; the subjects were approaching their last phase, moving toward their meet.

I still didn't believe they'd come into either of these dead-end alleys. It was too soon. They would fail outright if they shortened their SDR this much.

A small noise skittered to my left, deep in the black abyss of the dead-end, hitting me like the arrival of a hunter close-in while I drank from the pond. I started. Almost jumped, ran, and bounded away.

A rat, no doubt, feeding on the constant detritus of garbage littering Venice. Thousands must lurk in these warrens. All fat. Where were the cats?

Shit. Hold it together, Ben.

And more shit: it smelled like shit in here.

Crap. I'd just lost observation of the intersections. I re-established focus, could see both of them: the one, eight-feet ahead, to Calle Curnis; and the other, forty-feet distant, at the Calle… Rugheta.

My night vision had peaked by now; I'd be able to see my prey at a distance.

Hell. Where, pray tell, were they?

How long had it been? I dared not check my watch.

Waiting.

More waiting.

Had they doubled back? A standard SDR tactic. Which would mean Monica and I *would* fail outright.

Waiting.

I had a hunch.

Patience, Ben.

The breeze overhead vacuumed the air up from the maze of Venice's alleys. I supposed it'd smell much worse in here, otherwise. The wind was strengthening and it caused a fluting noise overhead, as it threaded over and through the roof tiles all around. Comforting. I never mind additional sound-masking.

Except the wind, moving the clouds along, opened a patch of clear sky, letting in the cold light of the evening's half-moon.

I was naked all of a sudden. *Shit.* Terror and panic. The light lit me like a spotlight. I knew our subjects' night vision must be as acute as mine by now. I slinked deeper into the alley, another short two feet, but enough to feel safer; the deer now hiding behind a tree next to the pond.

The scene had become almost day-bright. I shrank into myself as our two faux Ivans emerged into view at the intersection to the Rugheta.

They continued on. Towards me.

Two more clicks over the comms: targets re-acquired. A single click in reply.

My hunch had been correct. They'd stopped to observe, become accustomed to the environment's ambients, and let their own night vision deepen. A good tactic. It's what Monica and I would've done. They knew they were clean. I'd give them a point for it in the AAR.

I both froze and relaxed at the same time. If I showed the vaguest movement, they'd snap to it. To me. Blow my cover. *Crap,* I hoped that fat rat kept quiet. Keep gnawing on whatever you found, my friend.

They approached. Medium speed. Talking quietly and gesturing with their hands. And yes, looking around and behind as they approached Calle Curnis.

Breathe. *Breathe tidally, Ben.*

They arrived at the corner, perhaps ten-feet from me. I made out their faces clearly, and re-ID'd them as our two subjects. It's a tiny bit reassuring to know you're still surveilling the right folks.

I heard them only vaguely, but their lip movements were distinct. The combination helped me understand, as one mouthed, *"Ya neznayu."* I knew enough basic Russian to know it meant, 'I don't know.'

Good job, I thought. They were playing their cover one-hundred percent. Another point in the AAR.

Still, their SDR had proven ineffective because they'd didn't know they were being surveilled.

After they turned and progressed twenty feet away, I gave Moni two more clicks. I needed to move out; I'd take a parallel route to leapfrog.

Okay. I was done for the next fifteen seconds. A well-deserved sigh of relief.

I stood up as they faded into the dark, crept out, south down the alley from which they'd come. I'd loop east then north, waiting for a verbal report from Brigetti.

I'd drank enough water; it was time to leave the pond behind.

CHAPTER FOUR
Blown

Blown

Camp Peary's main drag, Donovan's Way runs north, almost to the edge of the York River. It dead-ends a hundred yards short of the water in a tight clearing of ancient oaks and chestnut trees. The clearing contains a trio of fifty foot long Quonset huts nestled in peaceful repose, although their memory contains the blood, sweat, and anguish of graduated and failed CO candidates over decades of aspiration to spydom. Donovan's Way... everyone knew, and each Case Officer candidate was taught, from the pre-dawn beginning of training up until graduation: everything was to be executed Donovan's way. Donovan's way or the highway. Simply put, if you didn't learn and practice your tasks with zeal, and obsess on everything until it all became part of your heart, you'd get invited to go home. Skip GO and do not collect 200 dollars. A no-brainer, for sure, but the road's title remained an eternal, poignant reminder.

On this late July evening, the warm air was filled with humidity, yet was made comfortable by the rising breeze coming off the Chesapeake to the east, and carrying with it a faint tinge of salt air. Behind one building was attached a lanai built from teak, with tiki torches providing a flickering, soft glow under trellises intertwined with climbing Wisteria and Finger Bush vine blossoms. The purple and orange flowers lent a tropical, sweet tang to the evening.

A few of the training cadre sat to one side playing traditional Hawai'ian music. Nothing I recognized; I vaguely recognized the cadre, though. They led a class behind us. They were apparently long-term Operations Officers of the Far East and Pacific Division. They must have spent significant time at Station Honolulu or Station Hilo at some point. Regardless, they sported aloha shirts, fresh leis, and sunglasses, despite the dim, flickering lamps. I was curious about the instruments they played—it's in the DNA by now—and had been granted a tour of their Ukuleles—standard—an Ipu—a type of gourd drum—and an Ohe Hanu Ihu, otherwise known as a bamboo nose flute. Yes, played from one nostril while fingering the short tube's note holes. It made a throaty, nasal melody. I did *not* want to know what came out when it was cleaned. That's what curiosity gets you in our trade.

Monica Brigetti and I were both halfway through our third Hawai'ian Hammer cocktails at this faux diplomatic reception, among the twenty-plus other CO candidates of our class. We were over halfway through the basic course and still striving to blow each other's covers—discover someone's true name, station in life, and pecking order in the grand machine. I was still Sam Richards to everyone, including Monica, although Monica Brigetti was her true name—but more about that later.

We'd each received a role to play for tonight's function, a background legend to act out, while attempting to glean intelligence from everyone else, standard fare for a dip reception. I was roleplaying an Army major in the Security Assistance Office of our facility in Honolulu and had also been given guidelines about what info I should divulge, depending on what buttons other diplomats pushed in me. Maybe I should just hang out in a shadowed corner and play orchid wallflower. Not authorized; that would cause severe negative points. You were required to socialize and elicit as much intel from as many other functionaries as possible. Then type up your report—*reports*—the very same night. Yes, you were scored; yes, it was a competition. And yes, it went into your class rank. We're just slightly competitive in this business. The lowest scorer of the night would get railed on by the entire cadre in front of the class. And if he or she really bombed, they'd send him back into the Attitude Chamber for a refresher in verbal and emotional torture, naked in front of everyone as the shrinks tore apart his mama's boy psyche and pointed out his lack of virility. It's not the sort of thing you want to experience more than the one, requisite time.

Enough happy thoughts, Ben.

The drinks weren't weak, and we were required to continue imbibing. The reasons were at least fourfold: the cadre needed to assess how we tolerated alcohol, if we drank too eagerly and how open we became after consumption; they assessed our elicitation techniques as the inebriation progressed, whether we needed to visit the restroom too often; how closely we stuck to our own covers and instructions for the event; and most importantly, how much we remembered from our elicitations—how much of the intel made it into our reports, accuracy, objectivity. All the usual.

I did enjoy the Hawai'ian Hammers, though, that's for sure.

I enjoyed Monica's company too, except I needed to circulate more, collect more intel. Maybe spill my drink on one of the cadre. You don't receive extra credit if your alcohol tolerance is so low that you vomit all over the Chief Instructor.

"Good hunting, Tina," her cover name, I whispered, as I moved off.

Which she returned with a gleaming smile under her soft, warm amber eyes under tresses of long chestnut.

I smiled to myself, chuckled.

One of the simpler traits to discover about fellow CO candidates was what language, or languages, they spoke. The info tended to come out over time, in little slips. I myself tended to curse in Russian; it gave everyone the impression I was some shit-hot linguist destined for Station Moscow. To them, I knew zero German or Czech.

The games were fun.

I sidled up to a pair of recent university graduates swilling their own Hammers, working on subtle slurs.

"Kak vashiy xhooiy?" I asked. More Russian swearing, 'How are your dicks?' or 'How's it hangin'?' I prided myself on the inside for being a consummate trouble-maker. An agent provocateur.

We compared notes, and I listened to each of them working their elicitation techniques on each other. Hey, if there's something to learn, I'll steal from anyone.

A waiter in white jacket and black bowtie circled with a tray of canapes. The three of us partook, and I managed to grab up two of them in one hand. They tasted great, and the extra protein and fat helped keep some of the ethanol at bay.

Yum. Smoked salmon over kiwi with cucumber sauce and a dab of cottage cheese. No idea what they were called. So I asked, because if either of these college boys knew, it would provide a lead-in to more elicitation and learning more of their real identities.

Another hour of circulating, talking, and listening, as the torches dimmed, the breezed grew, and the hula music faded.

* * *

We sat together, huddled over the small round table in her dorm room. Dorm room: *ha.* It was spartan, even sterile. Not by design, but by choice. We maintained our training covers at all costs; the penalty not to do so meant failure, at best getting recycled into a future class. The cadre might have required us to outfit our rooms with accoutrements consistent with our covers, except the effort was deemed too much of a distraction, sapping the energy needed for the myriad of learning tasks. Scuttlebutt was that it'd been a requirement in the past but had indeed led to poorer learning. Only a handful of CO candidates in each class succeeded... during the height of the Cold War, when we needed sufficient numbers of COs in the field to thwart the evil Red Horde.

I didn't understand why Tina Jergensen's room was a single. Most of us were in pair's rooms, with utilitarian bed, desk, and military-style wall locker. Tina, being assigned a single, obviously indicated seniority of some sort. She should have opted for a double, down with the rest of us serfs. But no, and I thought I knew why: she hadn't been allowed to, the thought being she should be that much better because of her seniority and seasoned experience. Good enough to fend off everyone's elicitation advances. Give her a negative handicap, right when the starting gate opened.

I thought it was bullshit. If a CO candidate couldn't discern, from Tina's sophisticated demeanor and poise, her seniority, he shouldn't be permitted to graduate—not even get recycled.

We hunched over a chaotic miasma of maps, SECRET satellite photos, tourist guides, train schedules, locations and running times of the *vaporetti* and *motoscafi*, and an untold number of resources about Venice's anatomy and metabolism. We dissected her, bit by bit, cramming every fiber of tissue and cell of her into our B-12 megadosed memories. We'd had last night and tonight, only after each evening's mock diplomatic function and typing of reports, to digest and memorize all this crap. We'd deploy tomorrow, a train up to New York to an early evening B747 over the pond to Milan. But there'd be no time for the haute couture shops; we'd need to find the first train available, through Verona and Padua, direct to Venice. And we wouldn't travel together, either as business associates, lovers, or a married couple. Strictly solo on the infil.

I'd completed typing my four reports in just over an hour. Speed and quality of typing were a key to success in this high-speed-chase, silenced 9mm, James Bond trade. Time loomed like the tall, black-robed fellow with a scythe. I then visited Tina, for us to finish our memorization exercises and planning. I suppose when you've been around long enough to attain the rank of lieutenant colonel in the U. S. Air Force, you're expected to type well—oops, more about that in a little bit.

We had no idea what type of operations we were planning for; we needed to prepare for every contingency. We'd receive our mission and its parameters sometime after we arrived. The exercise might be anything or nothing. Perhaps, Monica and I had performed so well we were being rewarded with the trip—a mission was to travel there and write a review of all Venecia's *gelatti*.

Not likely, Ben.

'Tina' welcomed me to her small room with a vibrant smile, a deft flick of her chestnut tresses, and a flash of amber eyes. I'd brought one half of our Venice materials, and she was retrieving her set from a desk drawer, certain to lock it afterward.

I couldn't resist being drawn to such beauty and elegance. Why had the cadre paired us together? Test my self-restraint? See if I could behaved under temptation? Test my self-restraint? Determine whether I could concentrate despite the provocative distraction? Or were they testing her on some deep dark behavior in her own closet? No way to know, and useless to speculate.

We kept things professional, and I fended off her flirting as best I could. It helped immensely when I finally realized she wasn't trying, wasn't acting. It was just her nature. Besides, she was way out of my league. Nevermind.

No time for amusements, Ben.

Back to business.

"These smaller canals, around San Polo Square would be good spots to change travel mode, either foot to a *gondola* or vice versa," I added. We especially needed to remember the location of all the canal bridges. They were critical choke-points as well as essential movement nodes, and were sparse in many areas.

"Yes, and I think at some point, we'll need to split up, change appearances, and conduct extra countersurveillance. We'll leapfrog each other with the trailing element checking for ticks," she replied. "Since we'll have comms, we'll need to take full advantage of them."

"Along with the requisite running rally points should our comms fail, right?" I asked.

"Yeah, and double-check the batteries."

"Or we may end up getting jammed, even though our sets are digital."

We smiled at each other, un-hunching ourselves and sitting back in our chairs. Time for a stretch. Things were going well, even though 'no plan ever survives the first contact of battle.' We worked well together. Maybe that's why the training cadre had paired us. See what we'd come up with working together. What they could develop us into.

No idea. I was making assumptions. We all know what that leads to.

"I bet this training op's just going to be another SDR, to acclimate us to another foreign operating environment." I posited.

"Watch it, Sam. The mission's liable to be anything. Something other than a CS exercise. Curveballs are stock in trade in our business, and for good reason."

"You're right. There I go again. Let's finish this section of the eastern curve of the Grand Canal, then call it a night." Personally, I thought our trip would be an operation to conduct surveillance on one or more of our classmates. We'd been concentrating on surveillance training for the last week. I checked my watch, the time now approaching 0100 hours.

"Oh crap. I'm out of coffee," as she went over to the machine on the corner of her desk. "Do you want some? I'll make a fresh pot."

This was usual when we worked into the night. I expected it. Was waiting for it.

"Yeah, that'd help. But don't trouble yourself. I'll go to the common area and get us a couple of mugs. There's always a pot there." A huge positive of the Agency was its resources. Almost unlimited. Coffee was more than plentiful. The only resource totally lacking was time. Never enough time.

Beta

Yeah, and a distinct lack of sanity.

"Thanks, Sam. That'd be a big help. Wait. Hang on a sec. Let me go. I need to get my blood moving. You young guys can go all night."

I was *not* about to ask her what she meant by that. Besides, she wasn't old at all, mid-thirties, only ten years older.

"Okay. Sure." The cogs between my ears accelerating.

"Just see what other highlights you can dissect from the San Polo district." And she exited, the door clicking shut with finality behind her.

Finality? Yes, finality for her, I thought, as I stood and moved over to her desk, pulling the small set of slender steel probes from a hidden compartment in my waistband. I knew her that well by now, understood how this mouse navigated its maze.

But shit, it took over a minute to violate the tumblers of her desk's center drawer.

I didn't bother to lock it afterward.

It wouldn't matter.

Back to the maps and sat photos, hunched over, with a huge grin on my face.

Maybe I should keep it. Make a beeline for the Chief Instructor's office. Give him a present.

"I remembered. Just black, right?" as she gently placed the oversized mug in front of me.

Then, "What's so funny, Sam?" sliding into the chair opposite me.

"So," I intoned.

"What?" A smile under her quizzical amber eyes, probing me.

"Lieutenant Colonel Monica Brigetti, of the United States Air Force," and I held up my trophy, displaying her own military ID card to her.

CHAPTER FIVE
Water

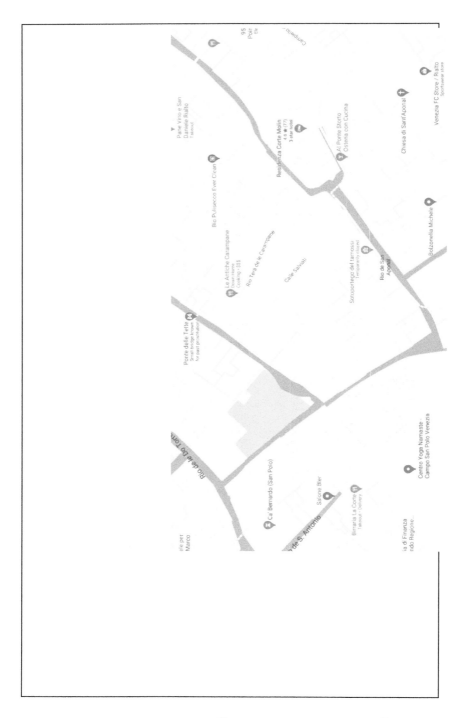

Water

The next fifteen minutes under Venice's dark, humid sky occupied Monica and me with more leapfrogging and waiting, leapfrogging and waiting, as she maintained a discrete trail on our pair of Ivans while I circled to the east, then north. Our quarry constantly kept their options open, ready to dart in any direction, or double, at the multitude of intersections rife within the San Polo district. At one point, Monica attempted to parallel their track and turned into a long dead-end. It was one of the few in-depth details I remembered—I don't like dead-ends, either literally or figuratively—so I reminded her of it just after she'd comm'd that she'd turned into it. She quickly doubled back to resume the tail, but our loss of target-lock caused my adrenaline to spike; we might lose them at any next instant.

After I'd blown her cover—hell, just two nights ago—she'd leapt at me over the small table, causing it to topple over, on top of us, as we both went down, and all the maps, photos, guides, and everything exploded in the space over us.

Shit.

It became like playing Twister and Fifty-Two Pickup at the same time. But not so funny, as she slammed an armbar across my throat and ripped at her ID card. I held it as far away as possible in my left hand.

"You fucking bastard, Richards!" she hissed, between clenched teeth.

We grappled like two Gila monsters trying to lock onto the other, thrashing around on the thin carpet of her modest room.

"*Wait.* Tina, I'm not going to—"

Shit. She was trying to bury her knee into my groin, missed, thank God, but struck deep into the inside of my right thigh. Crap, enough to stun a sinus in the femoral artery. My right leg went dead.

No time for chit-chat, I guess.

Not to mention the crashing din we were making at almost 2 a.m. The rooms were fairly soundproof, but not to the extent we were smashing at things.

"Give me my ID, you fucking bastard!" as she increased the pressure on my larynx.

My hips and one leg still worked, along with my right arm. My eyes worked, too, and I caught sight of one of the table's support legs.

A pause of almost a half-second, and she took advantage of it. Panther-quick, she hooked with her other hand at my face, connecting only halfway with a power rake as I spasmed away. Curling my body into the move I intended, twisting and propelling her mass away from me.

Into the table, where she struck the side of her head and was stunned.

Her pending gila lock on me slackened a fraction, and I bounced back from the move, twisting the other way, up and over, then on top of her, pinning her as she shook her head to regain full faculties. She writhed as I pinned her under me, just like on the playground in school, sitting on her chest with a knee on each bicep and my hands clamped around her wrists.

Hey, whatever works…

"Sam, I swear—"

"Monica, I'm not going to out you to the cadre."

"You shit bastard. What the fuck are you saying?" her writhing easing a bit.

"I needed to see if I could do it. It wasn't about you. It was about me."

"Then let me the fuck up, you scumbag."

"Okay, okay," as I gently rose and backed away.

She leapt up, again cat-quick, and I raised my hands in surrender.

I still held her ID, so pressed it forward. Disarm her with what she needed in the first place. She snatched at it, inspecting to see how badly I'd mauled it.

Then I announced, "Ben Daniels. Nice to meet you." and I presented my hand for a handshake.

Which she slapped away, and turned to upright her table. I went to retrieve the two capsized chairs.

So I'd reciprocated by telling her my own true name. I knew I'd need to. It was about trust. I'd gifted her the same leverage over me that I'd just stolen from her. I wasn't about to inform her, however—she'd just been bested, after all—how I was a mere staff sergeant in a rival service.

Even though your drawers are locked, it doesn't mean an enterprising miscreant can't sneak into them when you're not looking, or had been lured into a coffee run.

"They're moving into the greenspace off Rio Tera Aponal," Monica reported.

"Roger, I'll continue north to the next intersection." Which was actually a canal bridge over the narrow Rio de Beccarie. I held at the threshold of the bridge to observe the canal. Conditions were improving somewhat; more cloud breaks provided better visibility under the warm moonlight. The extra light would give us an advantage because our counterparts had to move in the open, whereas we could hide behind corners and such.

"They're pausing again," she said.

"I copy." It helped to catch my breath. I glanced up and down the canal, a deep, narrow chasm of shadow inside its sheer walls. Very few people traveled about the area; it lacked shops and eateries.

After another minute, "They're hopping a *gondola*."

Again?

"Can you see what direction they're headed?"

"The driver's on the east end of the *gondola*, toward you, so they'll move west."

Shit. Here we go again. We needed to trail them through the alleyways above the canal. Pursuit via *gondola* in the tight canal would be too conspicuous. Except it was barely a consolation that we'd planned for this. We were fortunate the *gondole* here were motor-less.

What followed became an exhausting, frustrating endeavor not to lose sight of our quarry. I was out of position to leapfrog even one bit. I needed to find a route through these warrens, just to catch up. All while remaining inconspicuous to the casual pedestrians, the area was sparsely populated, except a few locals still moving about. It wouldn't do to run—literally—into a pair of *carabinieri*; it might shorten my surveillance run.

Meanwhile, Monica trailed them from in front, deliberately

selecting the sparse bridge points to maintain discrete surveillance.

"I'm paralleling on Rio Terà Apona. There's a bridge a hundred feet ahead," she reported.

"Roger. I'm moving parallel on the north side." I found the Calle dei Botteri and turned west. The alley broadened here, peopled by the odd shops and takeout eateries. The going was smooth, and I kept to its southern edge to remain in shadow whenever the moon broke overhead.

"They're twenty feet past the bridge."

"Isn't there a canal-level path after your bridge?" I asked.

"Yes, Ben. I'm ten feet down-along already. Shut up and catch up."

I'd stated more than the obvious, and she'd called me on it. I don't suppose I should try to inform her of what she was already doing; it was sheer stupidity.

The surveillance became tedious, grueling, and wore on us. I double-checked the time: four hours in by now.

"I'm at the second bridge, at the Ramo Del Magazen. They're turning south at the canal's intersection, right in front of me."

Shit. I needed to move. I was losing track of the layout and the names of everything. *Crap.* I'd need to rely on Moni; with Italian as her native tongue, she memorized it all much faster.

Oh, there she was. At least it looked like her, back to me, but tall and slender. I was nearing the end of the canal-level path approaching her bridge.

"Where are you, Ben?"

Striding up silently, I grasped her shoulder. "Right here—"

And I was spinning, thrown and pushed all at once, then the heel of a mule kick in my chest as the brick wall behind me catches me just below the buttocks like a fulcrum, and I lever over backward flipping down and trying to roll around to land on my front and use my arms to help cushion the blow but it's water fifteen feet below and I—

"Monica—bpp—ppb—bppp—" as I go into and under the dirty water, pitch black and warm, oily.

I thrashed, turned myself over, then upright, head above the water, still sputtering as I treaded water in the dark canyon—the narrower canals in the lagoon were ten to fifteen feet deep—and wiped the stinging water from my eyes. Not as bad as diesel fuel…

an impression flashing in my head.

"Motherfu—"

"Oh, Ben. I'm so sorry," Monica whispered. My comms still worked—waterproof.

My head cleared, along with my eyes. *Crap.* How long had this taken? As much as five seconds? Six?

"Get after them, Moni," I hissed back. "I'm fine."

"Yes. Okay. I'm moving."

Breathing easier now, I regained my bearings. One immediate thought of the only thing to do, so I moved off in a broad breaststroke toward the T-intersection, forty feet ahead. My adrenaline supercharged, and I needed to smooth out my strokes to avoid splashing. Our target may not hear me, but a casual pedestrian could, then raise a hue and cry. *That* noise our classmates *would* pick up. The adrenaline sharpened the mind too—why couldn't I have stirred more of the juice before? Note for the future.

Need to do better, Ben.

The alley plan of the area crystallized in my head as I approached the corner.

"You'll have to reach the second bridge; they've been out of sight for too long," I pleaded.

"Shit. Yeah. You're right. Got it."

Obviously, she felt as flustered as I'd been twenty seconds ago. Another reason we operate in pairs; these things happen. She'd return to top form within the next five or ten seconds. Shit invariably happens. The key is to recover, lightning-quick.

It smelled of wet masonry and a tinge of fungus down here. I lurked less than a foot-and-a-half below the canal-level paths. I paused at the corner, suspicious about what I might find. They could pause again; blow me as I paddled towards their position. For all I knew, they'd halted for a *cannoli* break.

Nothing around the corner, and as another cloud break opened, I could make out the first bridge less than twenty feet to my front. I thought I saw a moving gondola—center of the canal—another thirty feet distant. Because it was white, or light-colored. Another blatant error in tradecraft. I'd make sure to ding them on it in the AAR. Especially because I wasn't feeling overly charitable at the moment; who knew what microscopic critters were chewing on me.

I moved off, smooth long strokes. "Are you there yet?"

"Almost."

What did 'almost' mean? She still sounded flustered. Yeah, a couple of things were at stake here, but she needed to focus on the present, not a brief minute in the past.

"It's okay, Moni. Relax. Don't panic."

Panic is a killer. Always. It's the most contagious emotion of all.

"Say, have you heard the one about the two COs who went to Italy for the Olympic event in canal diving?" Then I realized I needed to change my own attitude, too. Back to the moment, myself.

"Okay. I'm here. I've attained the second bridge."

That was more like it. Back in control and using proper terminology again.

"I've reacquired the targets. They're drifting, closer to you than me."

"Roger. I've got them. Thirty feet at my twelve o'clock."

Both our blood pressures must have dropped forty or fifty points in the last ten seconds.

"What are they doing?"

"Looking around again. They're preparing for another move."

Just so long as they didn't go for a swim. We had *not* planned for that contingency. Another note for the future.

"They're drifting to the western side. I think I make out a narrow ingress between two buildings.

"Roger," I responded. My foundering in the oily warmth transformed into a lovely evening swim, under the seductive, winking moon of the warm waters of a Mediterranean resort.

Well, not quite.

"That's it. They're debarking," she reported. "I'm moving across, to the southeast corner of San Polo square."

I knew it. Since they'd been going in this general direction since the Terraza Sommeriva, it was logical they'd traverse Sano Polo's open area. They could cross it directly and stop in the darkest shadows of one of the square's exits, or they might split up, circumscribe its perimeter, and each take up station in separate exits. Waiting and watching.

Brigetti and I had been surveilling for over four hours by now. How they behaved at this stage should prove an indicator whether they were nearing their meet.

The *gondola* had moved off. I took its place, raising myself inch-by-inch to peek over the edge at ground level. Our Ivans were thirty feet in, almost at the square. I sank back down and keyed my comms. "They're entering the square in about ten seconds."

"Roger," came her terse reply. "I'm in situ."

"Let me know when I can follow," I asked.

After another twenty seconds, "Okay, Ben. You're clear."

Thank Christ. I'd had enough of treading water in this warm, murky soup. I raised up smoothly, surmounted the edge, quiet as the first salamander emerging from the primordial ooze, stood, and moved in.

And pulled up short, almost cursed out loud.

Shit.

My shoes squished and squeaked. I was suddenly back in junior high school with a fresh pair of sneakers on the bare linoleum.

I ought to throw Brigetti into the drink, I thought.

Enough bullshit, Ben. Pull it together.

I removed my shoes and stowed them in a compartment of my jacket. But there was no way I'd remove the socks. I'd end up tripping on a raised cobblestone and rip off a nail.

I kept moving.

"They're headed directly across, to the southwest exit," Monica reported.

"How fast?"

"With purpose, I'd say. The square is empty."

This is it, I thought. We were moving into the last phase. Unless she was reporting only what her subconscious wanted to see. You always need to stay on top of yourself in our business. Otherwise, once again, poor tradecraft on their part, signaling intent. Except I couldn't be certain, I wasn't in there with her.

"Okay, this should be it," I replied. "I'm moving up. Can you leapfrog?"

"Yes. I'll move north to the other western exit and take the Calle dei Saoneri."

Another canal, a broad one, ran north-south, a hundred feet

west of San Polo. Two bridges spanned it from the square. Moni would use the northern one. I'd trail the pair across on the southern one. Unless their goal was this side of the bridge.

But I didn't think so. It didn't feel right.

My socks barely squished, although they left a trail of wet footprints in the dark. Which felt more than uncomfortable; if they doubled back, they'd easily pick up the trail of the wet ghost following them. Track me down. We don't like fluorescent arrows pointing to our position.

Shit.

Time to place a call to Saint Joshua.

I had to proceed slower than Moni could; I stayed at least forty feet back. I could barely see them under the low cloud cover. I checked to see whether a cloud break was approaching. I'd need to check every ten seconds or so. The wind sweeping the alleys chilled me inside my wet, dripping clothes. It was invigorating, though, and I was thankful; it would speed drying.

I needed to stay close enough to see which way they went at the next intersection. Monica would be in position at an intersection to the north by now, ready to react based on my next report.

The Ivans continued past the alley to the right. "I'm at Calle Seconda. Are they turning north, toward me?"

"Negative. They're moving on."

"Roger. I'm coming down."

Time for her to follow and for me to leapfrog. Once again, things became difficult, grueling. This was too much. The concentration and squinting demands were taxing. I needed to continually move my sight off-center to pick up my prey in the more rod-sensitive areas of the retinae.

"They're turning left," I reported.

"I'm coming up on you. Don't dump me into a canal."

"Haha." We were both confident the training cadre were monitoring our encrypted comms. It's always a given. You need to ignore it—too much of a bullshit distraction. Except I imagined the cadre were piqued by our use of each other's true names. That *would* become a huge distraction.

But I appreciated her humor. It helped keep things fresh during the appalling concentration effort.

She came up behind and passed by. I moved off to the south, then turned east to find a parallel track.

We both saw them as they turned west again, from the Rio Terà Nomboli onto Calle de Scaleter. I found Calle Corner as my parallel route and moved south. We were a hundred yards north of the Grand Canal in a densely packed *quartiere*.

What followed was an appalling series of fits and starts around corners and down short alleys. Highly advanced surveillance tradecraft for CO candidates, comprising flits and halts, whispered comms with hands over mouths, shrinking into crouches, sometimes even fully prone on the cool, bumpy cobbles.

After five turns, they came to an extended stop in the garden behind a *palazzo*. Monica and I huddled together to the northeast on the Calle Centani, just at the verge of the garden. It was large, about eighty feet by forty, indicating the importance of this *palazzo*. The Grand Canal was on the other side of it. This close to the canal, more foot traffic was evident.

Which Monica noticed at once, stood me up and pushed me against the rough brick of the building behind me, then smothered me with a full-body embrace.

CHAPTER SIX
Gondola under the Summer Moon

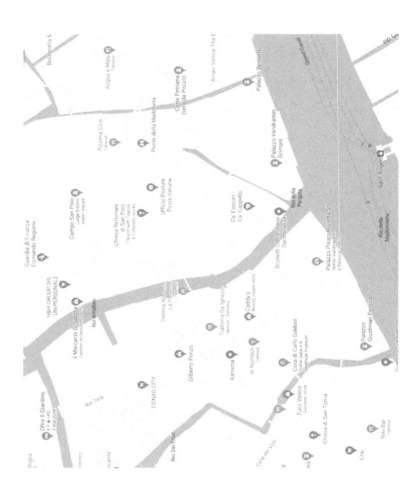

Gondola under the Summer Moon

Great.

No, not really, I suppose it gave us adequate cover, and no one passing by would raise a stink about a passionate Italian woman.

"Why, you're hardly damp anymore," she breathed.

"Sure. I was feeling much better. Well, up until this very moment," I whispered.

"What's the matter, Ben? Bashful? I know for a fact you're not shy."

"Shhh," I whispered. "I need to keep an eye on our guys." Then, "They've moved to a bench and they're just sitting there. Observing their surroundings. Maybe this is it."

"I don't think waiting in the open, if it's a meet, makes for good tradecraft."

"Yeah. Maybe the underside of the bench is a dead drop."

"Indeed. If they move off, we'll need to stay on them."

"Do you think we'll be able to tell from their behavior whether they've serviced the drop?" I asked.

"Yes. I should think so. Especially given the shit moves they've pulled so far." Good, she'd noted at all too. "Probably not right away, at their immediate egress, but shortly after," as she pulled me closer again.

Her cloying scent, radiant heat, and statuesque beauty invaded my very fiber, distracting me to thoughts of perdition. She was that powerful, and I lost sight of our quarry. Lost *all* focus as my blood began to flush me, and I became lightheaded.

"Monica—"

"Why, Ben. I never knew you cared," she taunted.

Apparently, I did, and my body cared even more. I pushed away slightly, abashed by the excessive stirring in my loins.

"Shit, Brigetti. We can still blow this op. Stop fucking around."

Mother of God!

No time for chit-chat, Ben.

She nudged me with an elbow, "They're still just sitting," after she risked a glance.

I followed her gaze as the cloud cover broke, bathing the lush garden. I notice how the pair continued to look around.

"I doubt the bench is a drop," regaining my composure. "They'd have left by now."

"Yes. I agree. But they must be close to their target."

We waited. The appalling surveillance up to this point now replaced by obsessive impatience. Still, the pause gave us time to rest, catch up, consolidate our thoughts.

"I need to put on my shoes. Keep an eye out," as I retreated a couple of steps and double-knotted the laces after cinching my feet extra tight. Your feet had best be in order when it's time to dance.

Monica tugged at me.

The pair rose and went straight for the *palazzo* door.

Excitement rushed in and the adrenaline spiked again—had a mind of its own by now.

They weren't very good. The pair struggled over the lock for at least three minutes, and only after the second one became impatient and replaced himself at the lockpicks.

I was really going to enjoy the After Action Review.

"If they suck this bad at locks, there's no way they'll relock it behind themselves," I commented. We both knew European locks didn't have turn bolts in the interior.

Despite their fumbling, they remained dead-silent, gained ingress, and closed the door behind themselves silently. I thanked Saint Joshua, because the outer and inner doors didn't squeak.

I couldn't stand it any longer. I moved in, along the garden's east edge to the *palazzo's* rear wall, then crept along it towards the door. I should have waited to see if they re-emerged as a tradecraft feint, except I felt an overwhelming urge to catch them.

I listened at the door. The ambients outside were weak, raising my confidence that the lack of sound from inside was accurate. Monica joined me, and I gave her the thumbs-up. She reached for the door handle.

Then my two functioning brain cells spoke up over my impatience. "Wait. They'll have to take time for their eyes to adjust going into the pitch-black after the moonlight out here." What I lacked in elegance and poise, I tried to make up for with tactical proficiency.

"Right," I wonder how they found this abandoned palazzo?"

Beta

she asked.

"I'll bet the cadre found it."

After another minute, I whispered, "Let's go."

She slowly operated the latch handle and inched open the outer, filigreed iron door. I placed my ear against the thick ornate wood of the inner door. Vague, distant thumping came through, fading. Distinctly footfalls.

"Footsteps. They're moving away from the door." I pulled the door towards me into its frame to release the jamb's tension on the bolt. Operated the handle, snail-slow.

We needed to enter quietly and quickly. The opening of a structure's door causes changes to internal sound pathways and ambient pressures. For the discerning and well-trained, you sense it at the threshold of your consciousness.

I pressed the door open, a crack... pause... listen... open it halfway, and move in, out of the way and let Monica follow, gently latching the outer one and moving in as I swing the inner door to, deliberately operating the handle in reverse.

We waited.

Didn't breathe.

Reached out with our senses in the pitch dark.

Waited for our eyes to adjust.

I moved them around, trying to distinguish anything across the entire area of the retinae. Swiveled my head for auditory clues and their direction.

Faint scraping.

Above.

Her lips to my ear, soft breathing saying, "Hear that? Upstairs?"

I gave her wrist two quick squeezes. Affirmative.

We stood in a small alcove, with a hallway leading towards the building's front; a set of narrow service stairs coalesced out of the blackness to our right.

My mouth to her ear, "The footsteps sounded sharp rather than regular. They went upstairs." Both of them? I wondered.

Two squeezes to my wrist as she began her climb, feeling out with her hands on the steps.

I followed in kind.

Slowly, like a pair of sloths on the ground, on all fours, as they climb back up their tree. I felt the stair steps, made from stone. Deathly silent. We like that when we're the hunters.

Saint Joshua had delivered again. Hell, I'll take it whenever I can.

My eyes had mostly adjusted. I could see Monica's black silhouette over the less black background. There must be windows, unblinded, on the second floor, letting in the ambient night illumination.

She stopped below the second floor's landing. I halted too, but placed a hand on her ankle to let her know I was right here. She raised her head in infinite degrees to observe the second floor.

I heard two clicks in my comms as she continued up.

The adrenaline coursed, heart pounded, and blood sang in my ears. My senses were jacked, and full night-vision had returned. I heard every cockroach in the distance, smelled the very stones and wood of the doors and furniture.

We were succeeding. The excitement inside the zone overtook me. We were about to catch the 'bad guys.'

I reached the landing. Moni was swiveling her head around.

She reached back and grabbed my wrist, pulled me forward.

The area was more than a landing; it was a spacious atrium, with the far wall made of large glass panes. Beyond them a roof garden.

It was easy to discern the space…

Flashlights.

This wasn't just poor tradecraft. It amounted to a cardinal sin.

Flashlights. *Shit.* I hate the fucking things. Not as much as dogs, but the bright beams tend to give you away when they shine on you, they telegraph the position of the bearer, and when you confront torch carriers, all they do is shine the bloody things in your eyes.

They were clearly at their destination. But doing what? If they were loading a dead drop, they wouldn't be searching for it. If they were servicing one that was already loaded, it might make sense. No, not really. Not at all; we're trained to feel around, even in the pitch-black. Besides, a cloud break couldn't be far off. Was it part of their instructions from the cadre, to do this?

Speculation was useless.

We had a job to do.

"Do you want to flip a coin for it? I whisper-asked.

"No, I'll go first," Monica answered. "But let's wait until they focus on a single spot together."

"Yeah, good idea."

We waited, as the beams crisscrossed the night garden, illuminated bushes, and benches in a totally un-choreographed dance, searched around, under things.

We waited. Accompanied only by each other's tidal breathing and mounting anxiousness. Time dilated. The clock slowed, as the torch beams moved in a slow-motion ballet.

"I'm going to go first, Moni. I need to confront these stupid assholes."

"Okay. Have it your way. I'll slip in behind you and flank to the right."

The glass-paned door stood in the middle of the garden's side, about thirty feet long, maybe fifteen deep.

I took deep, cleansing breaths, energizing the organism as I worked up the adrenaline to a fever pitch.

A cloud break as the pair knelt in the far corner around a small shrub.

I moved.

Closed my left eye and covered it with my hand. I kept the dominant side—the right—free.

Monica placed her hand on my right shoulder as I approached the door. She'd go in low and move around to the right, invisible now that our quarry had lost their night-vision and were in target-lock.

This was going to be fun.

Tunnel vision on the door handle as my right hand grasped it, tugged inward, and flung it against its metal stop, open 180 degrees.

BANG!!

Shotgun in the night.

I rushed in, full height, all puffed up. A Kodiak on its hind legs.

"Okay, you Ivans. You're in a shitload of trouble. Say, what have you got—?"

And both beams swept up from ground level and crashed into my face, lazing into my right eye, through to my brain in blinding pain.

It didn't matter. Monica maintained a bead on them. It was most important that both beams focused on me.

"Yeah, yeah. Hello to you too," I responded to their photon assault.

"Da shto?" one of them shouted.

"Yob' tvayu mat'!" from the other.

"Sure. Fuck your own mother," I replied. "You can drop the role-play. I'm from the class ahead of you"—don't say 'we,' Ben—"and your countersurveillance tradecraft is for shit. Oh, your SDR wasn't bad, but—"

And a flurry and a rush-in from the right, a thud ten feet to my front and the explosive bark of a gun firing.

Shit. What the fuck?

I dropped and rolled to my left, about two feet before hitting something hard, it digging into my lower ribs with a flash of red pain flaring in both eyes.

Guttural yelling from two males. A martial arts *'kiieaa'* exploding, must be from Brigetti.

Fuck.

Another gunshot. The bright flash blinding both eyes as I'd opened the left. It stank of cordite here, under the moon.

"Ben!"

I jumped up, followed the sound rushed in threw myself onto one of the flashlights I became all elbows and knees my own *'kiieaaa'* splitting the night, wrenched at the flashlight going for where a throat should be and getting it, clamping on the tracheal cartilage with all the sinew and adrenaline I could muster, pulled away the torch it was heavy, a foot-long, becoming a club in my left hand smashing where a head should be and making heavy contact swinging the second time and the raging homo sapien under me flung at me with his own adrenaline pushing and kicking, and another gunshot followed by an oomph and a scream but at least a male one as I rolled to the side and shined the beam up, Monica stood and I saw the gun in her hand pointing at the other male as he's jumping up ready to pounce on her, the other flashlight beam shining motionless, dead on the ground next to the black lump of a body.

"Stoi," Monica screamed, 'halt' in Russian.

Beta

The tall Russian fumbled and jumped into a run past Monica as I followed him with the beam as he zigged and zagged through the length of the rooftop garden and dove over the edge twenty feet down into the Grand Canal.

Monica was bent over the stout body, checking its pulse. My beam illuminated a growing black stain on its chest, about where the right ventricle would be, hiding inside.

Fuck.

My breath heaved. I began shaking.

Fuck this.

I found what looked like a 35mm film canister, pale white, lying near the bush. Pocketed it.

"Are you okay?" I hissed.

"Shit, Ben. These were real Russians. KGB."

"Are you okay?"

"Yes. Nothing from him, though. He's dead. I killed him."

What the fuck was this?

"Come on." I grabbed her and helped her up. Holding her. Supporting. "We've got to move."

"Yes. Help me, Ben. We need to CRITEG."—Critical Egress.

On the way out, I checked over the side, looking down at the Grand Canal. The cloud break illuminated a human form in a white gondola parked in front of the *palazzo*, limbs at severe angles and the head at an unnatural skew.

"Shit," as I doused the flashlight. The gunshot noises would have already drawn too much attention.

I wiped it off. No fingerprints, and dropped it into the canal.

"Give me that," and I gently pried the gun, a 9mm Makarov, from Monica's limp grasp, wiped it too, and dropped it overboard.

"We need to get out of here," I hissed.

I led her away as the cloud break slammed shut, engulfing us in darkness.

ABOUT THE AUTHOR

Dave Pendleton is a former national-level Human Intelligence—HUMINT—operator, with the Defense Intelligence Agency, and author of over 800 intelligence reports.

From budding automotive engineer to tri-lingual Army language specialist on the Cold War border, to assistant Army Attaché in Prague and Kiev working to counter weapons proliferation and illegal technology transfer, to Cornell grad student, and later corporate manager specializing in strategic planning, special projects, and geopolitical strategy, the CSCO series has been percolating in him for over two decades. He lives in Mooresville, North Carolina with his wife, Jenny. Their two adult sons, Daniel and Ben are out adventuring in the real world.